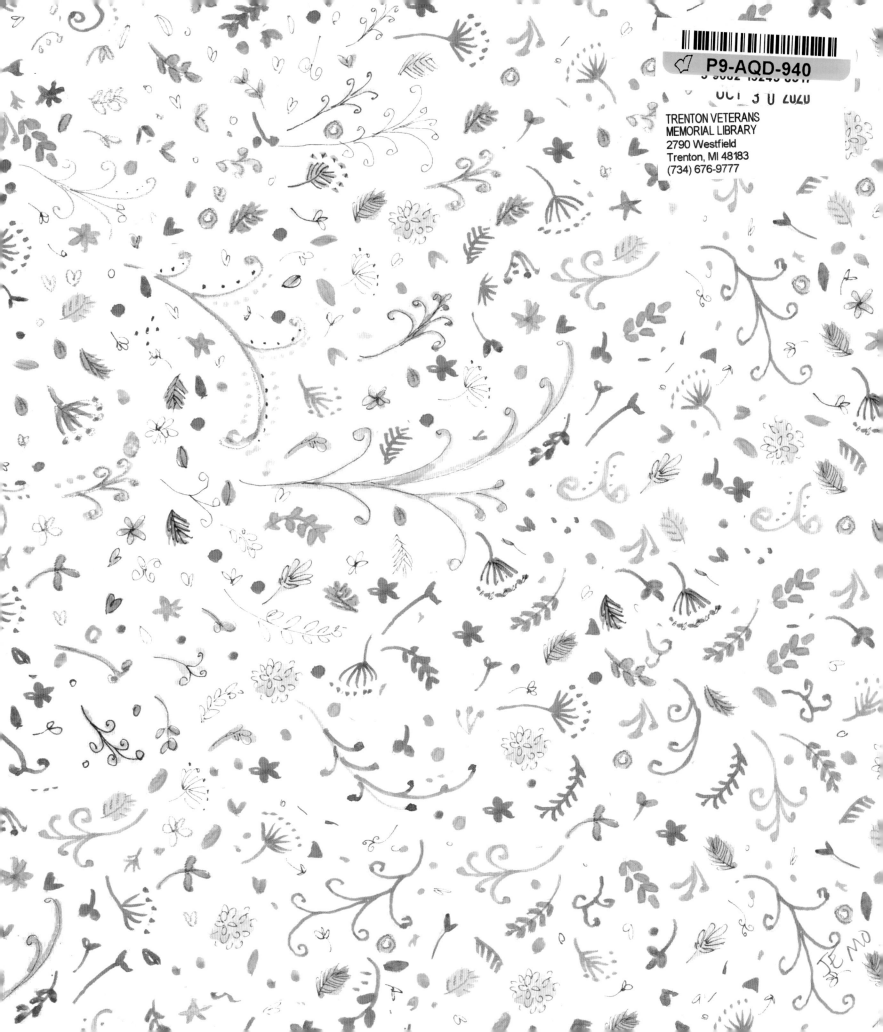

For my children, Ottilie, Rufus, and Agatha

BLOOMSBURY CHILDREN'S BOOKS
Bloomsbury Publishing Inc., part of Bloomsbury Publishing Plc
1385 Broadway, New York, NY 10018

BLOOMSBURY, BLOOMSBURY CHILDREN'S BOOKS, and the Diana logo are trademarks of Bloomsbury Publishing Plc

First published in the United States of America in October 2020
by Bloomsbury Children's Books

Bloomsbury books may be purchased for business or promotional use. For information on bulk purchases
please contact Macmillan Corporate and Premium Sales Department at specialmarkets@macmillan.com

Library of Congress Cataloging-in-Publication Data
Names: Morris, Lucy, author, illustrator.
Title: The song for everyone / by Lucy Morris.
Description: New York : Bloomsbury Children's Books, 2020.
Summary: A song coming from a small, high window transforms a lonely boy,
a stray cat, an elderly woman, then an entire town, so when the music stops,
they come together to save it.
Identifiers: LCCN 2020007109 (print) | LCCN 2020007110 (e-book)
ISBN 978-1-5476-0286-5 (hardcover) • ISBN 978-1-5476-0287-2 (e-book) • ISBN 978-1-5476-0288-9 (e-PDF)
Subjects: CYAC: Singing—Fiction. | Loneliness—Fiction. | Community life—Fiction.
Classification: LCC PZ7.1.M67276 Son 2020 (print) | LCC PZ7.1.M67276 (e-book) | DDC [E]—dc23
LC record available at https://lccn.loc.gov/2020007109

Art created with watercolor, pencil, pencil crayon, ink, and collage with digital manipulation
Typeset in Century Old Style Std
Book design by Jeanette Levy
Printed in China by Leo Paper Products, Heshan, Guangdong
2 4 6 8 10 9 7 5 3 1

All papers used by Bloomsbury Publishing Plc are natural, recyclable products made from wood grown in well-managed forests.
The manufacturing processes conform to the environmental regulations of the country of origin.

To find out more about our authors and books visit www.bloomsbury.com and sign up for our newsletters.

# The Song for Everyone

## Lucy Morris

BLOOMSBURY
CHILDREN'S BOOKS
NEW YORK LONDON OXFORD NEW DELHI SYDNEY

It was just a tiny window, too high in the eaves to be noticed from below and too small to let in much daylight.

And yet one morning out came a delicate tune.

A melody,

a song,

a sound so sweet

drifted out onto the breeze and down into the lanes below.

The schoolboy had a long and
lonely walk each morning.

As he passed beneath the small window
he stopped to listen to the music.

His loneliness instantly forgotten, he felt as light as a feather. The music and the delighted boy

bounced

away

together.

Nearby, the old lady hobbled slowly to town for bread and milk.
She felt the chill of the breeze in her aching bones.

As she walked, a trickle of notes tickled her ears. She rested
for a moment beneath the little window and listened.

The sound flowed down and wrapped itself around her weary body.

At that moment she felt so lively

and full of joy.

Tired and hungry, the cat from nowhere in particular took a nap in the afternoon sun.

Her ears pricked up at the delicate sound.

The music seemed to be whispering, "Little cat, little cat, follow me."

Notes dangled just out of reach and led her to the children
from Rose Lane who longed for a cat of their very own.

Over time it seemed that the music gave the townsfolk something they had been missing.

It searched out the lonely and lost, the needy and sad.

And above all, it made the people of the town care for
one another. They shared food and stories and kindnesses.

The days passed in peace and contentment.

Until one morning, without warning, the window was

completely

and utterly

silent.

All the townspeople woke feeling exhausted and grumpy.

The bread wouldn't rise, the milkman arrived late,
and the café owner simply stayed in bed.

Even the flowers drooped in their window boxes.

Why had the magical music stopped? What was to be
done? A meeting was called and the matter discussed.

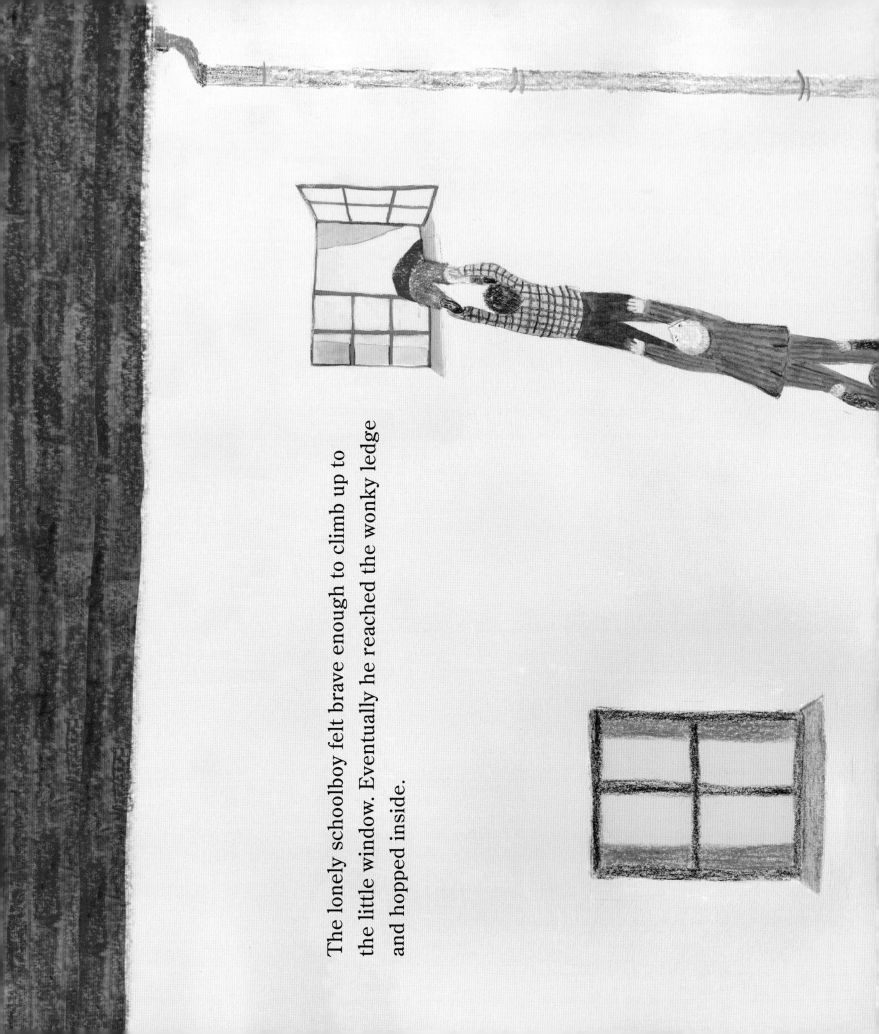

The lonely schoolboy felt brave enough to climb up to the little window. Eventually he reached the wonky ledge and hopped inside.

There in the dusty corner lay a tiny wren. She opened her beak but no sound escaped.

"It was just you singing for us?" he asked. "You must be so tired."

"I will help you," the boy whispered, and the little bird blinked back as though she understood every word.

The boy shouted down to the people below.

And everyone knew just what to do.

Two long days passed without a sound from the little window. The townspeople anxiously awaited even the slightest hint of a tune.

*Oh, what joy!*

A melody, a song. A sound so sweet.

It drifted out onto the breeze and down into the lanes below,
growing louder and more joyful with each beautiful note.

Everyone leapt from their beds and flew into the street, not
quite believing their ears. There in the little window stood
the boy and the wren making music together.

Singing the song for everyone.

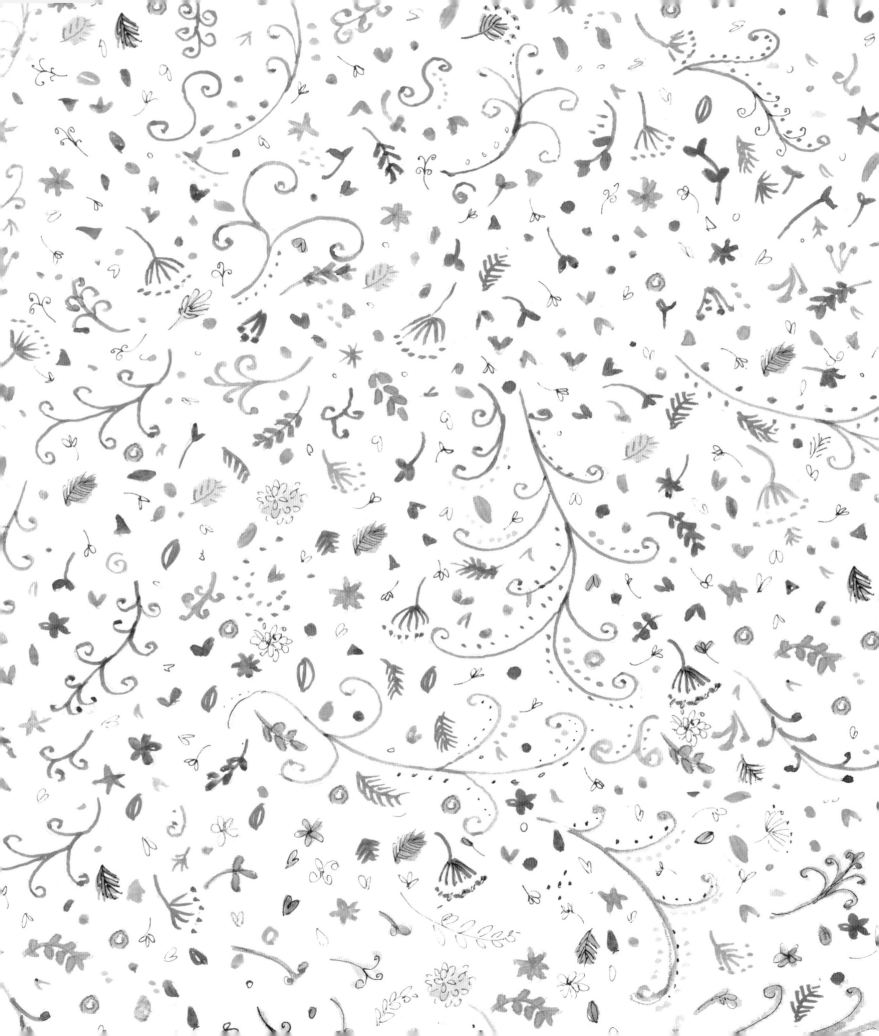